THE BRAVE SOCK MONKEY

By Fiona Rempt

Illustrated by
Noëlle Smit

A GOLDEN BOOK · NEW YORK

Translation copyright © 2013 by Rubinstein Publishing bv
Illustrations copyright © 2009 by Noëlle Smit
All rights reserved.
Published in the United States by Golden Books, an imprint of Random House Children's Books,
a division of Random House, Inc., 1745 Broadway, New York, NY 10019. Originally published in the
Netherlands in different form as *Rico Is Niet Bang* (*Rico Is Not Afraid*) by Rubinstein Publishing bv,
Amsterdam, in 2009, by arrangement with Random House Children's Books. Text copyright © 2009
by Fiona Rempt. Golden Books, A Golden Book, A Little Golden Book, the G colophon,
and the distinctive gold spine are registered trademarks of Random House, Inc.
randomhouse.com/kids
Educators and librarians, for a variety of teaching tools, visit us at
RHTeachersLibrarians.com
Library of Congress Control Number: 2012938940
ISBN: 978-0-375-86504-6
Printed in the United States of America
10 9 8 7 6 5 4 3
Random House Children's Books supports the First Amendment and celebrates the right to read.

One day in a faraway toy factory, a sock monkey was born.

As he was being stuffed and stitched, loud noises crashed around him, and machines swung and rocked him back and forth. The factory looked like a haunted house, but the little sock monkey was not afraid.

Finally, the day came when he was ready to leave the factory. He was tucked into a box and then put on a truck. The truck rumbled away.

It was so dark inside the sock monkey's box that he couldn't see his own hands, but he wasn't afraid. He even fell asleep as the truck drove through the night.

When the sock monkey woke up and his eyes got
used to the light, he found himself in a jungle full
of animals. A lion, a tiger, and a crocodile were all
watching him, but he was not afraid!

Then a pretty lady lifted him up and said, "Hello there, little sock monkey! Welcome to the toy store."

The next morning, when the
store opened, another lady came in.
She looked at all the toys—and then she took the sock
monkey's hand and gave him a big smile.

"Would you like to come home with me?" she asked
him. "Someone very special is waiting for you."

"How exciting!" thought the sock monkey. And he wasn't afraid, even when he was wrapped up in tissue paper.

Soon the sock monkey could hear lots of strange
noises: honking, talking, laughing, whistling, barking. . . .
These were outside noises, and of course the monkey had
never been outside. But he wasn't afraid. He even stuck
his nose through a little hole in the wrapping paper and
sniffed the fresh, cold air.

Then the sock monkey felt the crinkly tissue paper coming off.

He looked up to see a boy's two brown eyes gazing down at him. He'd never seen anything so beautiful!

The monkey felt himself
being squeezed very tightly.
It was his first hug.

"I'm going to call you
Rico!" said the boy.

Rico hugged the boy
back and put his head on
the boy's shoulder.

Rico and the boy instantly
became best friends.
They played the wildest
games. Even when Rico was
doing very difficult tricks,
he was absolutely
not afraid.

The boy never let Rico leave
his side. They were
always together.

As the boy
grew up, Rico
was more
and more
proud of him.

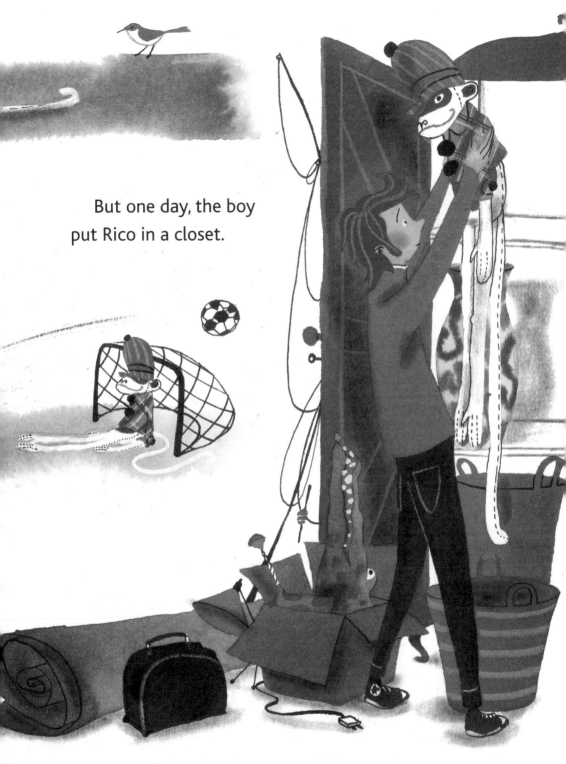

But one day, the boy
put Rico in a closet.

Poor Rico.

For the first time in his life, Rico was a bit scared. He was afraid of being alone.

Rico waited and waited. And then he fell asleep for a long, long time.

One day, the closet door finally opened.
Two brown eyes were looking down at Rico.
It was his old friend!

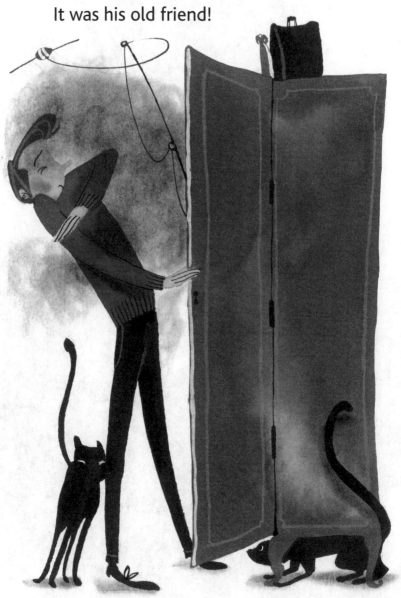

Rico was taken out of the closet . . . at last . . .

and was plopped into a washing machine. He got soaking wet, and a little dizzy, but he wasn't afraid.

After he was washed, he was hung up outside to dry. But he wasn't afraid then, either—he liked drying off in the warm sunshine and having his family around him again.

"Look at you, Rico! You're the bravest monkey in the whole world."

Two big green eyes gazed up at Rico . . .

and once again, he felt himself being squeezed very tightly. He knew he'd found a new best friend.

Rico was the happiest sock monkey in the world, and was afraid of almost nothing.